School of ROARS

Bestest Friends

pat a cake

When the stars come out
and it's night once more,
It's time to go to the School of Roars,
Wake up monsters and stretch your paws,
Jump up and go to the School of Roars!

It was another super-snufflesome night at the School of Roars.

"Good roaring, monsters!" said Miss Grizzlesniff. "Rooaarrrr!"
The monsters growled back as loudly as they could. "ROOAARRRR!"

Miss Grizzlesniff waggled a paintbrush in the air.
"Today we are going to do monster art!"

"Everyone pick a partner," said Miss Grizzlesniff. "I want you to draw around each other."

Wufflebump ran over to Yummble. Yummble was his bestest friend in the whole world! Wingston paired up with Icklewoo.

"Oh . . ." sighed Meepa.
She did not have a partner.

Yummble put his hand up.
"I can help Meepa after I've drawn around Wufflebump," he said.
Meepa grinned at him.

"Thanks!"

Miss Grizzlesniff got out some paper.

Wufflebump drew around Yummble,
then Yummble drew
around Wufflebump.

"Now you can decorate your pictures," said Miss Grizzlesniff.
"Yay!" cheered the monsters.

Meepa splatted her paper with paint splodges. It looked ROARSOME!
"Wow," gasped Yummble. "I'm going to splat pawprints, too!"

Yummble was so busy splatting with Meepa, he forgot all about his bestest friend. Wufflebump started to feel a bit sad.

When the bell rang, Miss Grizzlesniff sent the monsters out to wash their paws.

"Wait for me Yummble!" shouted Meepa.

Icklewoo and Wingston splashed about in one sink. Meepa and Yummble splashed about in another.

Wufflebump was left on his own. He started to feel VERY sad.

It was lunchtime, but Wufflebump didn't feel like eating.

"Do you want to swap my Slime Sandwich for your
Slurpberry Jelly?" said Meepa.
Wufflebump frowned. "No thanks."

"I'll swap my Scrumble Biscuits for it!" grinned Yummble, gobbling up Meepa's sandwich. "Yum yum!"

Yummble and Meepa laughed, but Wufflebump felt even sadder.

The monsters didn't have long to finish off their pictures before home time. The class worked very hard all after-moon.

Icklewoo coloured and Wingston swooshed his paintbrush.

Meepa took out one of the class spiders. It tiptoed all through the paint, across the floor . . . and up Yummble's arm!

Yummble roared with laughter.

"Ha! Ha! Ha!"

Miss Grizzlesniff clapped her hands.
"Now class," she said. "Let's have a look at
these monster-marvellous masterpieces!"

Icklewoo, Wingston, Meepa and Yummble all
held up their pictures. They were happy,
splatty works of art!

Wufflebump held up his picture. It did not look very happy at all.

"Oh, Wufflebump," said Miss Grizzlesniff. "What's the matter?"

Wufflebump sniffed. "Yummble used to be my bestest friend, but now he's Meepa's instead."

Poor Wufflebump.
Miss Grizzlesniff gave him a cuddle.

Yummble put down his picture.
"I'm sorry," he said. "I was having fun with Meepa,
but I wanted to have fun with you, too."

Wufflebump hadn't lost his friend after all.

"I'm your friend, too," said Meepa. "I did try and swap my
Slime Sandwich with you, but you didn't want to."
"Oh yes," blinked Wufflebump. "That's right!"

Miss Grizzlesniff unrolled an extra big piece of paper.
"Come on," she said. "You can all draw around me!"

Wufflebump couldn't stop smiling. He didn't just have one
bestest friend — he had a whole class full!

THE END

LOOK AND FIND

It's nice to have a special friend, but that doesn't mean that you can't be friends with other little monsters, too.

Meepa has invited Yummble and Wufflebump over for tea.
Can you find all of the little pictures hiding inside the big picture?

Point to every object that you see.

 Splatberries

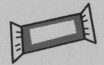 Fizzle Bar

 caterpillar

 saucepan

 orange